Big Trouble

by

S. P. Gates

Illustrated by Dylan Gibson

To Loz, Ali and Chris

First published in 2012 in Great Britain by
Barrington Stoke Ltd
18 Walker St, Edinburgh, EH3 7LP

www.barringtonstoke.co.uk

ISBN: 978-1-84299-837-3

Printed in China by Leo

Contents

1   "I Hate it Here!"   1

2   "Baboons are Big Trouble!"   8

3   "Keep Out of This, City Girl!"   16

4   The Rescue   22

5   Old One Eye   32

6   "I'm the Boss!"   38

Chapter 1
"I Hate it Here!"

Anna said to Levi, "This place is a dump."

"It isn't that bad!" said Levi. "I like our village!"

Anna was Levi's cousin. She lived in the big city. She had come to stay with Levi and his family for a few days.

"I hate it!" said Anna. "You have no water in your houses. You have to get water from a well! Your toilet is outside in a mud hut! And there's no McDonald's. I want to go home."

"But there's no bus back to the city until Friday," said Levi.

"You're kidding me!" Anna yelled at him. "I'm not staying here until then! I'd rather die!"

Anna was very upset and angry. She ran

outside.

"Where are you going?" Levi shouted after her. "You can't walk all the way back to the city!"

Outside, the village girls were sitting under a tree. They were chatting and having fun. They stopped when they saw Anna and looked at her hard.

"There's that snooty city girl," one of them said.

"I heard her call our village a dump," said another. "Who does she think she is?"

"She thinks she's a queen," said one who was called Sarah. "She thinks she's better than us."

Sarah got up and walked over to Anna.

"Go home, city girl," Sarah said. "We don't want you here."

Anna began to feel scared. Sarah was big and strong. She was the leader of the village girls.

"Stay away from me, Sarah!" Anna said, and took a step away.

But then they heard someone shouting. A woman raced into the village. It was Levi's mum. She had been out in the fields picking corn cobs.

"Hurry!" yelled Levi's mum. "The baboons are coming! They're coming to steal our corn!"

Chapter 2
"Baboons are Big Trouble!"

The village girls forgot about Anna. They went running into their houses. Soon they came out again with pots and pans.

Everyone in the village rushed to the fields with pots and pans. Some picked up sticks and rocks on the way.

Anna stared at them. What were they

doing?

Levi rushed past with a big pan. "What's going on?" Anna asked him. "Has everyone gone mad?"

"Come on!" shouted Levi. He grabbed her arm. "Baboons are big trouble! We've got to chase them away before they steal the corn in our fields!"

A gang of young baboons had come down from the hills. They'd got into the fields. They were going crazy, smashing down the corn plants and ripping off bits to eat.

"That's not so bad," said Levi when he saw them. "They're just little baboons. They'll be easy to scare."

"They don't look easy to scare to me,"
said Anna. The young baboons had big,
sharp teeth. They jumped around and
stamped their feet, screaming their heads
off all the time.

Levi said, "It's good their parents aren't
with them. Or Old One Eye."

"Who's Old One Eye?" asked Anna.

"He's the leader of the baboons," said
Levi. "He lost one eye in a fight. He's as
strong as a gorilla. He can rip a man apart.
And nothing scares him!"

All the people from Levi's village were making a big noise. They bashed their pots and pans with sticks. They yelled and shouted, even louder than the baboons.

The young baboons screamed back. They threw corn cobs at the people. But then they ran back to the hills.

"Look!" said Anna. "That one's got a baby on its back!"

"It must be its baby brother or sister," said Levi.

The baby baboon couldn't hang on. It fell off into the grass, under a tree. The young baboons ran off into the hills, leaving the baby behind.

"Kill it!" said Sarah. She picked up a rock.

Chapter 3
"Keep Out of This, City Girl!"

Sarah threw a rock. It missed the baby baboon. But the baby screamed. It ran up the tree and hid there. Sarah picked up another rock.

"I'll get it next time," said Sarah. "I just need to get closer."

Anna was very upset. She said, "Leave that baboon alone. That's cruel!"

But Sarah said, "Keep out of this, city girl! You don't understand."

Another girl said, "We hate baboons here. They steal our corn."

Sarah started to walk over to the tree where the baby was hiding.

Then Levi's mum said, "Don't go any closer, Sarah. A leopard sleeps in that tree. He might be there now."

Sarah dropped the rock. She came back to the fields. "I don't need to kill the baboon," she said. "The leopard will kill it for me."

Anna ran back to Levi's house. She sat on her bed, very upset and angry.

When Levi came back, she said, "How can Sarah be so cruel? She wants to kill baboons. Just because they steal corn cobs."

Levi said, "If baboons steal our corn we starve. Old people in the village die. Little kids die. That's why we hate baboons. You can't blame us."

Anna said, "But baboons have got to eat too! You can't blame them either!"

Anna started to cry.

Levi said, "Don't cry, Anna."

"I can't help it," said Anna. "I keep thinking about that poor little baby."

"That baby will be fine," said Levi. "Its mum and dad will come down from the hills to find it. Old One Eye might come."

"But what about that leopard?" said Anna.

Levi grinned. "Even leopards are scared of Old One Eye," he said.

Chapter 4
The Rescue

That night Anna couldn't sleep. She wondered, *What's happened to that baby baboon? Is it still in the tree? Have its parents been to find it? Has the leopard killed it?* She just had to find out.

So she sneaked out of the village and through the fields. She sneaked over to the

tree. It was a bright starry night. But it
was scary out here. Even more scary for a
city girl.

Scary noises came from up in the hills.
Wild animals were up there, hooting and
screaming.

Anna shivered. But she kept going. Now
she was under the tree. She looked up.
Something wet dripped on her face. Anna
wiped it off and looked at her hand.

"Oh no!" she thought. "It's blood!"

Was it the baby baboon's blood?

She looked up again. She saw a dead
deer up in the tree, with blood dripping from
it. The leopard had killed it and dragged it
up there.

But there was no leopard in the tree. He must be out hunting. But where was the baby baboon?

Then Anna heard a tiny scream. She saw the baby, hiding in the leaves.

"You're still alive!" said Anna.

She started to climb the tree to get the baby. She had to climb over the dead deer. She felt sick. Blood from the deer got on her dress. Then she heard a shout, from under the tree.

It was Levi. He'd seen her sneak out of the house. He'd followed her.

"You crazy girl!" said Levi. "Come down! Forget the baboon!"

"No!" said Anna. She grabbed the tiny baboon. It held on to her and wouldn't let go.

"Come down!" said Levi again. "That old leopard is around here somewhere! He will smell us!"

Anna climbed down with the baby. She and Levi went back towards the village.

All at once Levi stopped. "Stand very still," he said

Anna saw two golden eyes in the long grass. They glowed like fire.

"It's the leopard," whispered Levi. "He's hunting us."

"What do we do?"

"Run for your life!" said Levi.

They raced through the fields.

"Faster!" yelled Levi. "Run for the village!" He could hear snarls behind them. That leopard was close!

They ran faster, into the village. Then Anna fell down. "I can't run any more!" she sobbed.

Levi stopped running too. He looked back down the street.

"It's OK," he told her. "The leopard has gone. It won't dare come close to houses."

Anna stood up. The baby baboon was still holding on to her. "Are you all right?" Anna asked it.

"Never mind about the baboon!" Levi shouted. He was mad at Anna. "That leopard almost got us! Just let the baboon go! I told you baboons were big trouble!"

"OK," said Anna. She looked sad. "I'll let it go."

"Do you promise?" asked Levi.

"Yes, I promise," said Anna.

Chapter 5
Old One Eye

Something bit Levi's big toe hard. He opened his eyes. It was the baby baboon, sitting on the end of his bed.

"What are you doing here?" Levi yelled at it.

The baby baboon looked at Levi with big eyes. Then it gave him a hug and patted his head.

"Anna's right, you are cute," Levi told it. "Why are you still here?"

Levi went out of his bedroom. The baby baboon came too. It hung on to his neck and didn't let go.

Levi's family had gone to the market. Only Anna was in the house.

"You promised to let this baboon go!" said Levi.

"I know," said Anna. "But it was too hard. So I hid the baby baboon in my bedroom"

"What are you going to do with it?" asked Levi.

"I'm not going to leave it here," said Anna. "Sarah is so cruel. She'll kill it. I'm going to take it to the city. I'm going to keep it as a pet."

"You can't do that!" said Levi. "It's a wild animal. It doesn't belong in a house in the city! It belongs here."

"But I can't leave it here!" yelled Anna. "I'm the only one who cares about it! Give it to me!"

She snatched the baby from Levi.

Just then a loud screech came from outside the house.

Anna and Levi stopped yelling.

"What's that noise?" asked Anna. Her eyes were wide and scared.

Levi raced to the door and looked out.

"Someone else cares about that baby," he told Anna. "That's Old One Eye out there. He's come to find it."

Chapter 6
"I'm the Boss!"

Old One Eye had long, yellow teeth.
There was a red hole in his face where his
right eye had been. He had scars all over
his body. Many baboons had tried to fight
him, to take his place as leader. But Old One
Eye always won.

Now he yelled and beat his chest, as if to say, "I'm the boss!"

A rusty old car was parked in the street. Old One Eye ripped off a door and looked inside. The baby wasn't in there.

He jumped up and down on the car roof and screamed in rage. He tore apart a hen house. The hens flew everywhere.

Levi peeped out the door.

"He's smashing the place up looking for that baby!" he told Anna.

Then Old One Eye stopped. He sniffed the air.

"He knows the baby's close by," said Levi. "He can smell it."

The people had raced to their houses. They'd shut themselves inside. They knew when Old One Eye got mad, they were all in danger.

Just then, Levi said, "There's Sarah!"

Sarah had been to the river to get water.
She was carrying a can of it on her head.

Old One Eye screamed again. Sarah saw
him. She dropped her water can. Water
splashed everywhere. She ran into an
outside toilet.

But she wasn't safe there.

Old One Eye began to rip big holes in the mud walls of the toilet.

"Give me that baby, Anna!" said Levi.

"No!" said Anna, hugging the baby. "He's mine!"

"He's not yours," said Levi. "He belongs to his family."

"No," said Anna, and she hugged the baby closer. "Keep away!"

"If we don't give him back, Old One Eye will kill Sarah!" said Levi.

Anna didn't want to do it. But she handed the baby over.

"Stay here!" said Levi.

"No," said Anna. I'm coming too."

Levi didn't have time to argue.

Levi walked outside, with the baby baboon in his arms. Anna walked beside him. She was shaking with fear. But she wanted to make sure the baby was safe.

"Hey!" shouted Levi to Old One Eye.

Old One Eye stopped screaming. He stopped ripping the toilet hut apart. He turned round and saw Levi and Anna. He gave a roar of rage. But then he saw they had the baby.

Levi didn't go any closer to Old One Eye. That was far too risky. He put the baby on the ground. Sarah watched him through a hole in the toilet wall.

"Back off," Levi told Anna. "As slow as you can." They walked slowly backwards to Levi's house.

Old One Eye ran up to the baby. He
sniffed it. He picked it up.

"He'll hurt it!" said Anna.

"Shhhh! No, he won't," said Levi.

Old One Eye hugged the baby. He was
very gentle. Then another baboon came
running up. She'd been hiding in the corn
field. The baby jumped onto her. He held on
very tight. She hugged him and patted his
head.

"Bet that's his mum," said Levi.

"Look, they're going," said Anna.

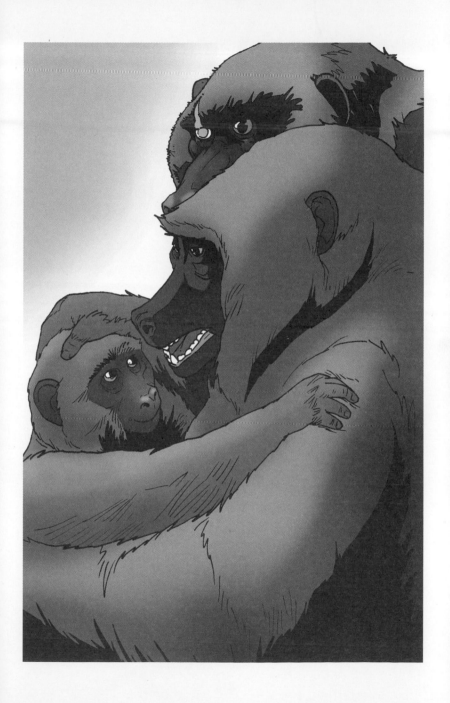

Old One Eye and the baby's mum trotted back to the hills. The baby was on its mum's back. Soon they vanished into the trees.

"Bye, baby," whispered Anna.

"Don't be sad," said Levi. "He's back where he belongs."

Now it was safe, Sarah came out of the toilet.

"That Sarah hates me," Anna told Levi.

But Sarah didn't hate Anna any more.

"You and Levi saved my life," she told Anna. "Old One Eye nearly killed me!"

The other village girls ran over to them.

"I was wrong about Anna," Sarah told them. "She is OK. For a city girl!"

The girls crowded round Anna. They smiled and asked her questions.

"We're going on a picnic this afternoon," Sarah told Anna. "Down to the river. Do you want to come along?"

"Yes," said Anna. "That would be good."

"Didn't you say you wanted to go back home?" Levi said to Anna. "Didn't you say you hated it here?"

"It's not as bad as all that," Anna told him. "I may even stay a bit longer."

"Come on," said Sarah to Anna. "You can help us get food ready."

Anna and the village girls chatted and giggled as they went off.

"Can't I come to the picnic?" Levi shouted to Sarah. "After all, I saved your life too."

"No!" Sarah yelled back. "Keep away! We don't want boys around. This picnic is for girls only!"

Levi shook his head and grinned. "Those girls," he said, loud enough for them to hear. "Sometimes they are the biggest trouble of all!"

Have you read Levi's other stories?

Levi is in danger. There's a killer croc on the loose – and it's hungry! Can he escape its jaws?

There's a snake in the pond and it's coming for Levi's brother. Can Levi save him?

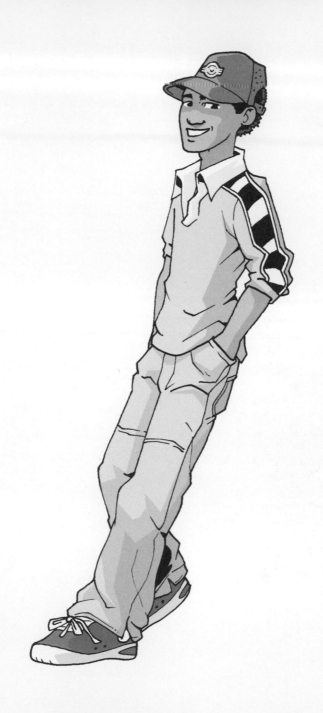

Bomb!
by
Jim Eldridge

The clock is ticking ...
Rob's a top bomb disposal
expert. He has to defuse a
bomb in a school before
it's too late.
Can he do it?

Take Two
by
Jo Cotterill

Max asks Carla and her
best friend Lily to the
prom. Instead of getting
mad, they decide to get
even. It's sure to be a night
Max will never forget!

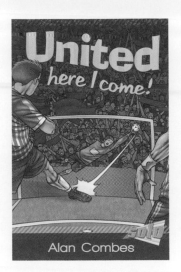

United Here I Come!
by
Alan Combes

Jack and Jimmy are very bad at football. But Jimmy is sure he will play for United one day.

Is Jimmy crazy — or will he get there?

Topspin
by
Sean Callery

Tim needs to learn the topspin serve to win the tennis final. But his dad is his tennis coach and he walks out on the family. Can Tim do it alone?

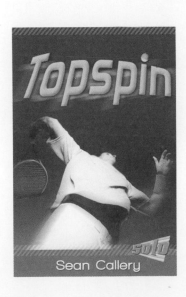

You can order these books directly from our website at
www.barringtonstoke.co.uk

Our books are tested
for children and young people by
children and young people.

Thanks to everyone who consulted on
a manuscript for their time and effort in
helping us to make our books better
for our readers.